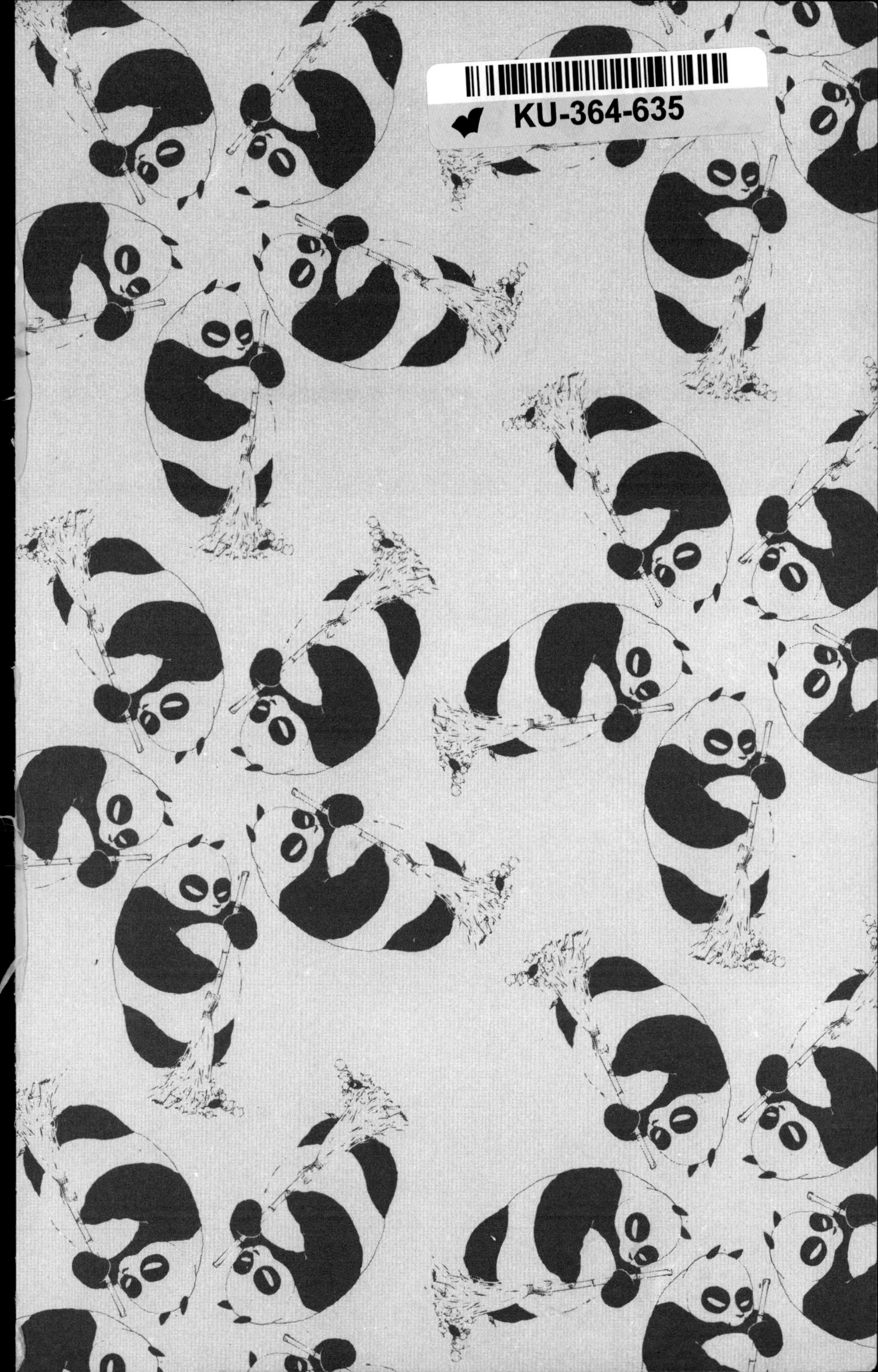

VIZ GRAPHIC NOVEL

RANMA 1/2™

8

This volume contains RANMA 1/2 PART FIVE
#1 through #6 in their entirety.

Story & Art by Rumiko Takahashi

English Adaptation by Gerard Jones & Toshifumi Yoshida
*

Touch-Up Art & Lettering/Wayne Truman
Cover Design/Viz Graphics
Editor/Trish Ledoux
Assistant Editors/Annette Roman & Toshifumi Yoshida
*

Editor-in-Chief/Satoru Fujii
Publisher/Seiji Horibuchi
*

First Published by Shogakukan, Inc. in Japan
*

Printed in Canada
*

Published by Viz Communications, Inc.
P.O. Box 77010
San Francisco, CA 94107
*

10 9 8 7 6 5 4 3 2 1
First printing, April 1997

VIZ GRAPHIC NOVEL

RANMA 1/2

STORY & ART BY

RUMIKO TAKAHASHI

CONTENTS

PART 1
"OKONOMIYAKI" MEANS "I LOVE YOU"

RRRRUUUMM
IT'S BEEN A LONG TIME, GENMA SAOTOME.
HMM... ?
HAVE WE MET BEFORE ?
DON'T PRETEND THAT YOU DON'T KNOW ME...
...UKYO!? THE ONE YOU LEFT BEHIND!?
VSSH
OKONOMIYAKI
U... UKYO !?

TENDO TRAINING HALL
WOW... POP GOT A LETTER OF CHALLENGE?
YES, AND A VERY STRANGE ONE AT THAT...

SEE?
meet me at the empty lot at 4 o'clock
A...A CHALLENGE...
...ON OKONOMIYAKI!?

KLAKKETA
KLAKKETA

HUH ?!
TP.
FZZZZZ
SSSZZZ
POP!
HEY POP!
KONK KONK KONK

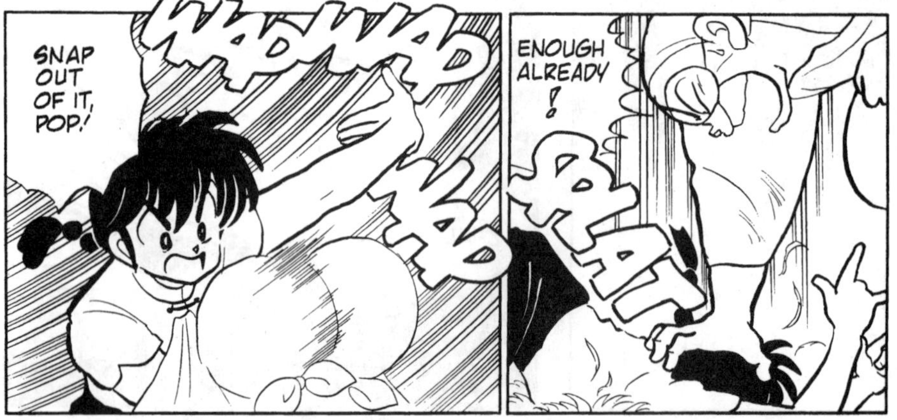
SNAP OUT OF IT, POP!
WAPWAP
WAP
ENOUGH ALREADY!
SPLAT

VZZZ
WHA--?!
TWONG
VEEN
VEEN
RANMA! NEXT IT'S YOUR TURN TO PAY!

YOU GOT THAT?!
HAHA-HAHA!

I'LL SEE YOU SOON!

COME BACK HERE, YOU!
VVVV

WHOA, BOY.
BOOM

LET IT GO...
...FOR YOUR OWN GOOD.

.....
THAT OKONOMIYAKI GUY...

I KEEP THINKING WE'VE MET BEFORE...
HMM...

HEY POP, HOW COME HE BEAT YOU SO EASY? YOU'RE HIDIN' SOMETHING, AREN'T YOU!?
.....

RANMA, CAN YOU...
...CAN YOU **PROMISE** ME THAT, NO MATTER **WHAT** I TELL YOU, YOU WON'T BE SHOCKED?

SURE.

THEN COME CLOSER.

THE TRUTH IS...
...THAT UKYO...

GAA!!

I CAN'T TELL YOU...YOU'RE TOO EASILY SHOCKED...
SPLOOSH
RRING RRING

WHP
WHP
WHP
MOOSH
STAY LIKE THAT FOREVER, FOR ALL I CARE!

I WONDER IF I SHOULD TELL HIM...?
BOP
WAP
GRARARA
OOLO

WHAT'D YOU WANT TO TALK TO ME ABOUT, AKANE?
RANMA... UMM...

YOU'RE AN ONLY CHILD, RIGHT...?
YEAH, WHAT OF IT?
WHAT IF YOU FOUND OUT YOU... WEREN'T?
WHAT ARE YOU TALKING ABOUT?
I HAPPENED TO OVERHEAR IT...
UKYO'S CHALLENGE!

FEEL THE WRATH OF THE CHILD YOU LEFT BEHIND!
FORGIVE ME! I WAS POOR! I COULD BARELY FEED RANMA AND MYSELF!

MR. SAOTOME... HAD AN ILLEGITIMATE CHILD !?

SO THAT'S IT!

AREN'T YOU SHOCKED ?
WHO, ME ?
BONK

NAH, I DIDN'T KNOW THE OLD GUY HAD IT IN 'IM! AND WITH HIS LOOKS, TOO!
JOG JOG

YOU PIG.
WHO SAYS I HAVE ILLEGITIMATE CHILDREN ?
OH NO? THEN WHAT WAS UKYO TALKING ABOUT?

CLASS, I'D LIKE TO INTRODUCE A NEW STUDENT...

SSSSSS
SSSSSS
SSSSSS
WHAM
WH-WHAT ELEGANT TECHNIQUE.
MURMUR
MURMUR
MY HOBBY'S MAKING OKONOMIYAKI... "JAPANESE PIZZA"!
SSSSS
SSSSSS
MY NAME'S UKYO KUONJI!
HUH?
UKYO?
HEY, THAT'S--
RANMA! IT'S BEEN A LONG TIME!
SHAH
I-IT'S ALL COMIN' BACK TO ME...
AH!
PAP

HEH.
SHIK!
YOU'RE... YOU'RE...

FOR TEN YEARS I'VE HUNTED YOU!
VSSH

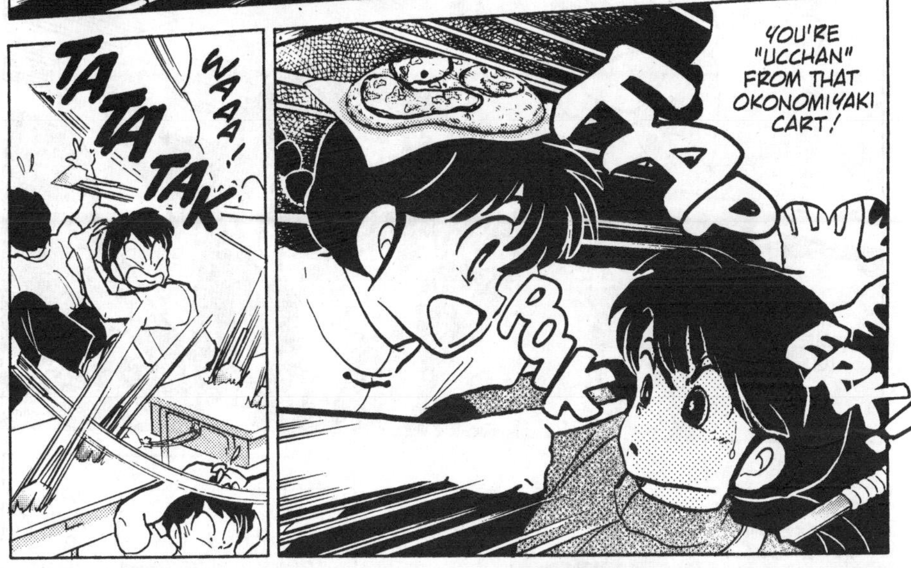
YOU'RE "UCCHAN" FROM THAT OKONOMIYAKI CART!
FLAP
ERK!!
TA TA TAK
WAAA!

YEAH! FOR A WHILE, ANYWAY.
OHH!
GASP
YOU WERE CHILDHOOD FRIENDS?

I MET UKYO WHEN POP AND I WERE TRAINING. "UCCHAN" WAS A NICKNAME I CAME UP WITH.
UCCHAN!
TA TA TA
COMIN' FER ANOTHER FREE MEAL, EH!? LITTLE PUNK.
GET RID OF HIM, UKYO.
SIZZLE
KONOMI
GOOD OLD UKYO...
GET READY!
THIS TIME...I WIN!

I GOT FREE OKONOMIYAKI PRACTICALLY EVERY DAY!
NAW! TAKE A LOOK.
ISN'T THAT CALLED "THEFT"...?

HE'D ALWAYS HAVE ONE HOT 'N' READY FOR ME.
UKYO USED TO DRAW LITTLE PICTURES WITH THE SAUCE!
IT WAS A SAD DAY WHEN I HAD TO GO...
A BEAUTIFUL FRIENDSHIP, BORN OF COMBAT!
WOW!
CAST YOUR MIND BACK TO THE DAY YOU LEFT.
WHAT ARE YOU SO MAD ABOUT?
HOW DARE YOU?!
BANG
BYE-BYE, UCCHAN! BYE-BYE!
VRRRR.
WELL, LET'S SEE...
YOU WERE RUNNING AFTER US, CRYING...

YOU SAID YOU'D TAKE ME WITH YOU!
YOU JERKS!
VRRRRRRRRRRRR
JERRRKS!
BYE-BYE, UCCHAN!
THE HUH...?
OH? SO THEN WHAT'S WITH THE "VRRRRRR"?
HUH!?
YOU'RE WRONG! UKYO'S FATHER GAVE IT TO ME!
BOOOM
MR. SAOTOME...?
AND THAT'S NOT THEFT?!
COME T' THINK OF IT, WHY THE HECK WERE WE TRAVELIN' ON YOUR OKONOMIYAKI CART?

I WAS SUPPOSED TO TAKE UKYO AS PART OF THE DEAL, BUT ALAS...
WHAT IS UKYO, A LITTER OF KITTENS ?!

YOU BROKE YOUR PROMISE...
...AND LEFT ME BEHIND.

BUT DIDN'T YOU HAVE YOUR OWN FATHER?
YEAH, WHY WOULD YOU WANT TO COME WITH MY STUPID OLD MAN?
!
MOOSH

RANMA...YOU REALLY DON'T KNOW?

WELL, WHO CARES? LET BYGONES BE BYGONES!
C'MON! BE A MAN!
PAP PAP
......

SO. AT LAST I UNDERSTAND...
SSSSS SSSSS
HUH ?

...HOW YOU FEEL !
WHSH

RANMA! I HAVE A SPECIAL RECIPE IN MIND FOR YOU!
PREPARE YOURSELF !
VMM
KREEEK
BAM

"MEET YOU AT THE FIELD BEHIND THE GYM AFTER SCHOOL..."
IT'S A CHALLENGE !
SOME GUYS JUST DON'T MAKE ANY SENSE...

PART 2
SAUCY REPLY

WE GOTTA SEE THIS!
I HEARD RANMA'S GOING TO FIGHT THE NEW KID!
YAMMER
YAMMER-YAMMER
CHECK OUT THE RING!
WHAT THE HECK?!
RANMA, PREPARE YOURSELF...
WHAT... WHAT IS IT?!
TUP
HIYA, UCCHAN.

WE ARE HERE... TO DUEL!
SQUENCH
SO STOP CALLING ME THAT NAME!
VUM
WHY NOT? I THOUGHT YOU LIKED IT WHEN I CALLED YOU THAT!

WHY CAN'T WE BE FRIENDS LIKE BEFORE?
THAP
YOU DARE CALL YOURSELF A FRIEND?

SOMETHING STILL BOTHERS ME.
THIS UKYO...
WHOA!
GASP
YEAH
GO!

BUT THE ONE WHO STOLE YOUR CART AND LEFT YOU IN THE DUST WAS MY POP, RIGHT?
SO WHY'RE YOU SO MAD AT M--
VSH
SHUT UP!
VSH
MR. SAOTOME...
IS THERE SOMETHING YOU'RE NOT TELLING US?
THERE IS.
DUM DUM

YOU'RE THE MOST STUBBORN *GUY* I'VE EVER MET.
THOP
WHY... YOU...

WA!
TAKE THIS!
VSH VSH

EEEE-OW!
HUH?
FAK
YOW!
WRRRRR
TK TK TK TK

COOK MINE OVER EASY!
WHOA!

KRAK

OOOOH!!
ALL AROUND THE RING... IT'S A GIANT HOT PLATE!
THIS IS INSANE!
NOW, FOR OKONOMIYAKI UKYO'S SPECIAL RECIPE...
I HOPE YOU LIKE IT!
FLA!
SHLORP...
YAA!!
PLAP PLAP
SSSS.

WHA--
?!
BLORBLE
YAA YAA
AND THIS...
MY SPECIAL BATTER... DEEP-DISH GLUE!
HYAH!
IS RUBBER YAKISOBA NOODLES!
FWONG
FWONG

VRRRR
BANG
BANG

HISSS
YEEOUCH!
GO!
GO!
OH, MAN... THAT YAKISOBA SMELLS GOOD!
MY MOM MAKES OKONOMIYAKI WITH THOSE NOODLES IN IT, TOO!
THAT RANMA'S MAKING ME HUNGRY!

H-HEY, COME ON, NOW!
I FORGOT TO OIL THE GRILL.
SSHHHHH
FLOOP
TONG

AND TO TOP IT OFF... TEMPURA FLAKES...
VOOM

...MIXED WITH GUNPOWDER !!
POOF
PAPA PAPA
PAPA PAPA PA PA PAPAPA PA PA
RANMA!
OH, MAN...
IS THIS IT...?
I'LL BE NICE... AND NOT SETTLE THIS...
...IN SUCH A DANGEROUS PLACE.
POP POP POP POP
!
SINCE WE...WERE FRIENDS ONCE...
GNNNN

FWAP
TWONG
SSS
SSS
YAAH!!!
BA!
THEY'RE TAKING IT OUT OF THE RING!

YEAH. WHY?

......
WELL? I'M WAITING.

MAYBE I SHOULD JUST SELL YOU TO A CIRCUS.
DUM DUM
WHADDA LOSE

BELOVED FRIENDS SINCE CHILDHOOD! WHY MUST THEY FIGHT EACH OTHER SO!?
OH, WHAT TRAGEDY!
BOOM

TATATATA
YOU SISSY!
GET BACK HERE, UKYO!
DA DA DA
ERG!
C'MON! FIGHT LIKE A MAN!
THOK
TAP
WHY, YOU--!
BOING

HYAA!
VISH
WAH!
I TRY TO BE NICE TO YOU AND WHAT DO YOU DO ?!
VOOP
YOU... YOU...
YOU GOT TO HAVE YOUR FUN ON THAT GRILL...
NOW IT'S MY TURN!
WAIT!
J-JUST A SECOND!
"WAIT" ?!
YOU'RE THE ONE...

...FORGET
THE
FLOUR!
POOF
BWAH!
NEVER...
BAKING
FLOUR
...WHO
STARTED
THIS
!
WH-WHAT'S
THAT
WHITE
SMOKE?!
IT'S BY THE
P.E.
EQUIPMENT
ROOM!
VROOM
KOFF
KOFF
AK!
AK!

WHY THAT LITTLE...
OF ALL THE DIRTY TRICKS...
hak hak

koff koff
koff

GOTCHA !!
GLOMP
OH...!
N?

SLAP
HANDS OFF!!
UH...
NOW WHAT ?!
'SCUSE ME...
ARE THOSE BREASTS... ?

PART 3
UKYO'S SECRET

THAT UKYO GUY... IS A GIRL ?!
A GIRL ?!
NO!
OOOH
GASP

..."CHILDHOOD FRIENDS"...
.....
MAYBE THEY'RE NOT JUST...
TH-THEN THE WAY SHE CAME HUNTING FOR RANMA...
YES, SO HE IS. SHE IS.
P.E. EQUIPMENT ROOM

.....
UKYO... UM...

YOU'RE... UH... YOU'RE...
SINCE WHEN...?
"SINCE... WHEN"?
WHAT KIND OF STUPID QUESTION IS--
UBBLE UBBLE UBBLE
EEEEEEEEE YAA!!
WHAAP
WHAT'S THE BIG IDEA?!
Y-YOU DON'T CHANGE BACK WITH HOT WATER...
DOES THE SIGHT OF CLEAVAGE MAKE YOU INSANE?!

BARRROOM
RANMA... YOU NEED TO MEET SOMEONE.

THIS IS UKYO... YOUR FIANCÉE!
HEH HEH
BOOM
TOK

DO TELL.
SPLORT

I WAS GOING TO OFFER MY OKONOMIYAKI CART AS THE DOWRY.

TWONG

BUT AREN'T PROMISES MEANT TO BE BROKEN?

ON THAT DAY, MY LIFE AS A WOMAN CAME TO AN END.

OOOOOO

AFTER THAT, ONLY ONE THING MATTERED TO ME...
HEARD THE LATEST? UKYO GOT DUMPED BY HER FIANCÉ.
NOT ONLY THAT, HE STOLE THE FAMILY BUSINESS, TOO.
PSST PSST PSST
TSK-TSK
NOW SHE'LL NEVER FIND A HUSBAND.
DEVOTING MY LIFE TO REVENGE!
BOOOM
OKONOMIYAKI BECAME MY LIFE-- I SET UP A PORTABLE GRIDDLE AND COOKED IT BY THE RAGING SEA!
DOOOOM
SIZZLE SIZZLE
BA!
UM...
WHY DID IT HAVE TO BE THE SEA?
ISN'T THAT KINDA POINTLESS?
THAT IS THE POINT, STUPID! DON'T YOU EVER WATCH SAMURAI MOVIES!?

......
NO WONDER SHE HATES THEM SO MUCH...
POOR GIRL...

SHE HAS EVERY RIGHT TO HATE.
SIGH
INDEED...

GO AHEAD, UKYO! TAKE OUT ALL YOUR ANGER ON RANMA!
FUNCH

AND HOW D'YOU FIGGER THAT!?
MOOSH
AFTER ALL, IT'S YOUR FAULT TOO!

DESPITE MY AGREEMENT WITH UKYO'S FATHER...
RANMA WAS ALREADY PROMISED TO MARRY AKANE.
P.E. ROOM
YET I DID NOT WANT TO GIVE UP THE OKONOMIYAKI CART.
BEING UNABLE TO MAKE THAT DECISION FOR HIM...
I HAD TO TRUST THE BOY TO CHOOSE ON HIS OWN.
WHA-?
HUH?
!
RANMA, YOU CHOSE AKANE EVEN BACK THEN...?
.....
I DON'T REMEMBER ANY OF THIS!

RANMA, M'BOY... LISTEN WELL AND ANSWER YOUR FATHER.
WHICH DO YOU LIKE BETTER? UKYO OR OKONOMIYAKI?
HMMM...
OKONOMIYAKI!
AND THAT ANSWER MADE THE DECISION FOR--
BONK
YES, SHE HAS EVERY RIGHT...
WAIT! WAIT! I DON'T EVEN REMEMBER ALL THAT!
WELL, REMEMBER THIS!!

GRRR
GRRR
ENEMIES TO ALL WOMEN!
"ENEMIES TO"...WAIT A MINUTE!
TALK ABOUT DYSFUNCTIONAL FAMILIES!
YOU TWO ARE DISGUSTING!

WELL, I GUESS THEY'VE GOT IT COMING.
WHAP
POOM

WE DON'T CARE!!
I DIDN'T EVEN KNOW UKYO WAS A GIRL TILL...
SCREE SCREE
BA-BONK

HUH?
UKYO'S GONE TOO.
HE'S ESCAPED!
RANMA'S GONE!
!

HEY!

VROOOOMM
WHERE DO YOU THINK YOU'RE GOING ?!
JUST FOLLOW ME.

THERE IT IS.

FWNG

HERE. YOUR SPATULA.
TAK.

I WON'T MAKE ANY EXCUSES.
DO WHAT YOU WANT TO ME.

HEH. ALL RIGHT THEN...
RRRR

EXPECT NO MERCY!
WHEN YOU ABANDONED ME...
KRAK
VMMMM
YOU MADE IT IMPOSSIBLE FOR ME TO EVER AGAIN EMBRACE MY OWN FEMININITY!
UH...
WHOA! DON'T YOU THINK YOU'RE OVERREACTING?
WATCH YOURSELF, RANMA...
VSH
VSH
SHUT UP!!
TAP
SINCE THAT DARK DAY...
VIP

...I'VE SWORN THAT I WILL NEVER...
SWAH

...LOVE ANOTHER MAN !!
DUCK
WHISH

A CUTE GIRL LIKE YOU.
WHAT A WASTE.
POK
ERRK

CYUH...

WHO'DVE THOUGHT LITTLE "UCCHAN" WOULD GROW UP SO CUTE?
BLUSH
CUTE...

TOO BAD NO GUY WILL EVER--
BOOM
YOU'RE LYING! I'M NOT CUTE!!
BLUSH

IT'S NOT A LIE. YOU ARE CU--
WHACK
VOOM
STOP IT!!
BLUSH

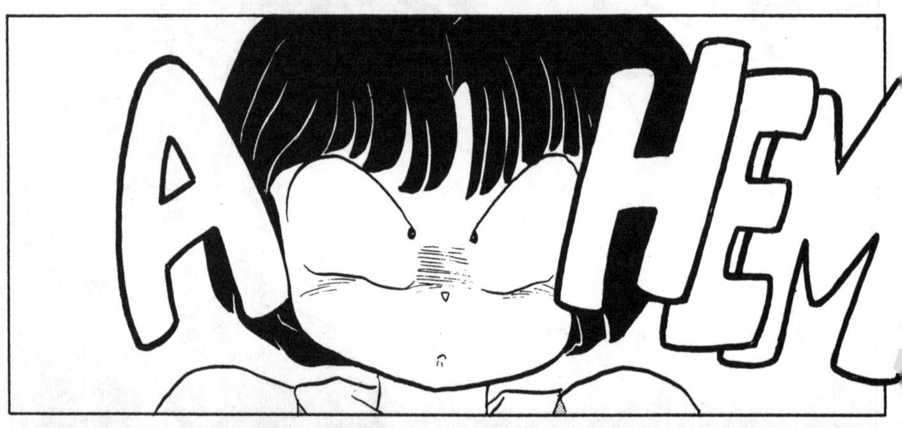
AHEM

WH-WHAT'S WITH YOU, AKANE?
YOU MUST BE HAPPY...NOW THAT YOU HAVE A CUTE FIANCÉE!

SO. YOU'RE AKANE.

YEP. CUTE FIANCÉE, MEET UNCUTE FIANCÉE.
PAT
S-S-SO WHAT...?

JAB
SO WHAT IF I'M NOT CUTE?!
TOMBOY!
JAB
.....

SO YOU TWO AREN'T GETTING ALONG?

GEE, IS IT THAT OBVIOUS!?
AM I RIGHT? UNCUTE OR WHAT?

PAP
WHSHH

LET'S BE FRIENDS AGAIN... STARTING TOMORROW!
LET'S LET BYGONES BE BYGONES, SHALL WE?
VVIP

UH... RIGHT...
YOU MUST BE VERY HAPPY.

PART 4
RYOGA VS. UKYO

'MORNING!
HEY, HEAR ABOUT RANMA?
WHAT, YOU MEAN HIS NEW FIANCÉE?
BLAH BLAH
EVERYONE'S TALKING ABOUT IT.
WHAT'RE YOU TALKING ABOUT?!
WHADDYA NEED TWO FOR!?
AIN'T YOU GOT ALL THE LUCK.
OH, SO?
I HAD ENOUGH PROBLEMS WITH JUST AN UNCUTE FIANCÉE!
THEN WHY DON'T YOU SWITCH TO THE CUTE ONE?!
VIP VIP
BOING, BOING

OOOM!

SPLAAAAT
OFFICIAL SOUVENIR KOUNTRY KILNS™ of JAPAN
MOOSH

UH... RYOGA... ?
HWOOOOO
AKANE...
GASP
OOOH!

I HEARD THE RUMORS.

RUMORS ?
YOU MEAN ABOUT THE OTHER FIANCÉE...?

IT'S OKAY. I DON'T CARE WHO RANMA GOES OUT WITH.
WHAT SHE SAID.
I WILL NOT HAVE IT!!
OH!
GAK!
CREEEK...
PSST! NO WAY!

EVEN IF THE OTHER FIANCÉE...

LOOKED LIKE THIS...
TEE HEE
GIGGLE
Flower
OR THIS...
MOOVING Sale

NOW YOU'VE DONE IT! NOBODY GETS AWAY WITH SAYIN' THAT I...
I WILL NOT SEE AKANE INSULTED BY A TWO-TIMING LOUT!
SHAA
SHAA

...WOULD GET ENGAGED TO SOME ANCIENT CLAY STATUE!

I WON'T STAND BY AND HAVE MY ENGAGEMENT RIDICULED!
YOW!
TAK TAK TAK.
WHSH WHSH
THAT VOICE...
HUH?
GYAA!
VOOSH
TAKE IT BACK!
UKYO!
GASP

I DON'T KNOW WHO YOU ARE-- BUT TO CHOOSE RANMA IS TO CHOOSE DEATH!
VOOM
RYOGA!
RANMA HAS AN ALLY, EH?
SO.
CHA
ZA

WOULD YOU HIT A GIRL!?
STOP!
WHA...?

A GIRL... !?
FEH.
SWAP
AS IF I DON'T KNOW A MAN WHEN I SEE ONE!
TANG
TWOK
TANG
WHAT ?!
WHO'RE YOU CALLING A MAN?! FLOUR BOMB!
BOOF
GWAH!
GOTCHA!
HIYAAA!

TAKE THIS !
VSSHH
ZUNG

AK...!
FWP...
OOOOH!

AHHH!
IT'S OVER!
RYOGA, DON'T--!
GULP!
BAZOOM
CHECK 'EM OUT. STILL THINK "HE" IS A GUY!?
EEP...
BOOM
GET LOST!
BACH
OOOH!
HEH.
HEY. DIDN'T I JUST SAVE YOU?
SHOWING MY CHEST TO ANOTHER MAN! YOUR OWN FIANCÉE!
OH, RYOGA...

SCHOOL NURSE
NN... ?
OH, THANK GOODNESS... HOW ARE YOU FEELING, RYOGA?

I'M SORRY. YOU GOT HURT BECAUSE OF ME...

N-NO...NOT REALLY. I DID IT ON MY OWN...
THANK YOU ANYWAY.

BABUMP
HUH ?

.....
BADUMP BADUMP BADUMP
.....
SOBB
AKANE !!

HEH HEH HEH.
POP

BIFF BAFF BOOM
AK!
UGH!! OOF!
HM ?

WOOM
RANMA HONEY...
WHAT WERE YOU THINKING !?
HMPH!
huf huf huf
SHOOP
HONESTLY!

ANYWAY, RYOGA...

DON'T WORRY ABOUT US.
WE'LL BE ALL RIGHT.

UH...
OH...

"DON'T WORRY
ABOUT US..."

SIGH.
AKANE...

"DON'T WORRY ABOUT US," SHE SAYS!? AAAAARGH!
BOOM BOOM BOOM
HEY HEY HEY!

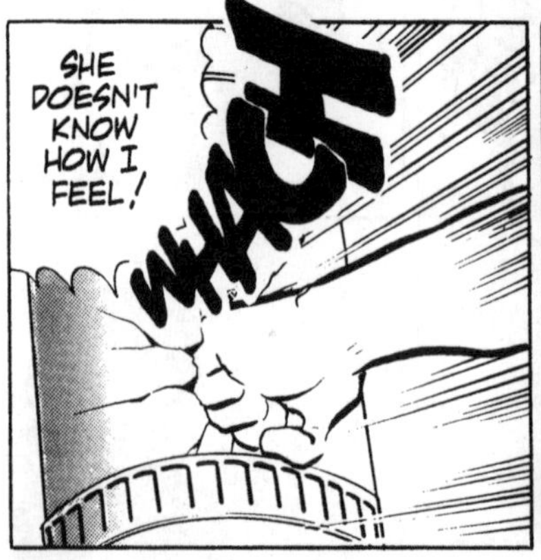
SHE DOESN'T KNOW HOW I FEEL!
WHACK

WHAT'S GOT YOU SO WORKED UP?
POST

YOU'RE IN LOVE WITH AKANE, AREN'T YOU.
WH...
ERK!

WHY... YOU... !
JAB
HOLD IT! I'M ON YOUR SIDE!

LET ME INTRODUCE MYSELF PROPERLY.
I'M UKYO... RANMA HONEY'S *CUTE* FIANCÉE.

OKONOMIYAKI UCCHAN'S
CHAN'S

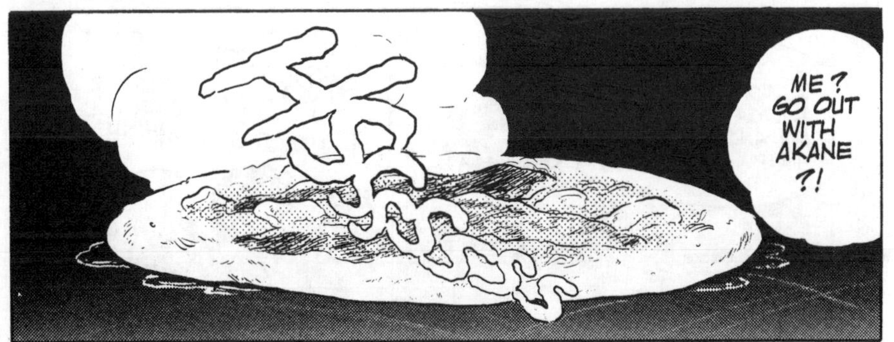
ME? GO OUT WITH AKANE ?!

I'LL SET IT UP FOR YOU!
FWIP
WHY? SHE'LL ONLY SAY NO ANYWAY.
MAYO

COWARD.
BAM
WHAT DID YOU SAY !?

THAT'S A HOT GRILL.

JUST LEAVE IT TO ME.
I PROMISE I'LL GET AKANE TO GO OUT WITH YOU.
SO, "PROMISE," EH...?

I WONDER IF RYOGA LEFT ON ANOTHER TRIP...
SOMETHIN' TELLS ME...
...HE'S A LOT CLOSER THAN YOU THINK.
KWEE KWEE KWEE

PART 5
LOVE LETTERS IN THE SAUCE

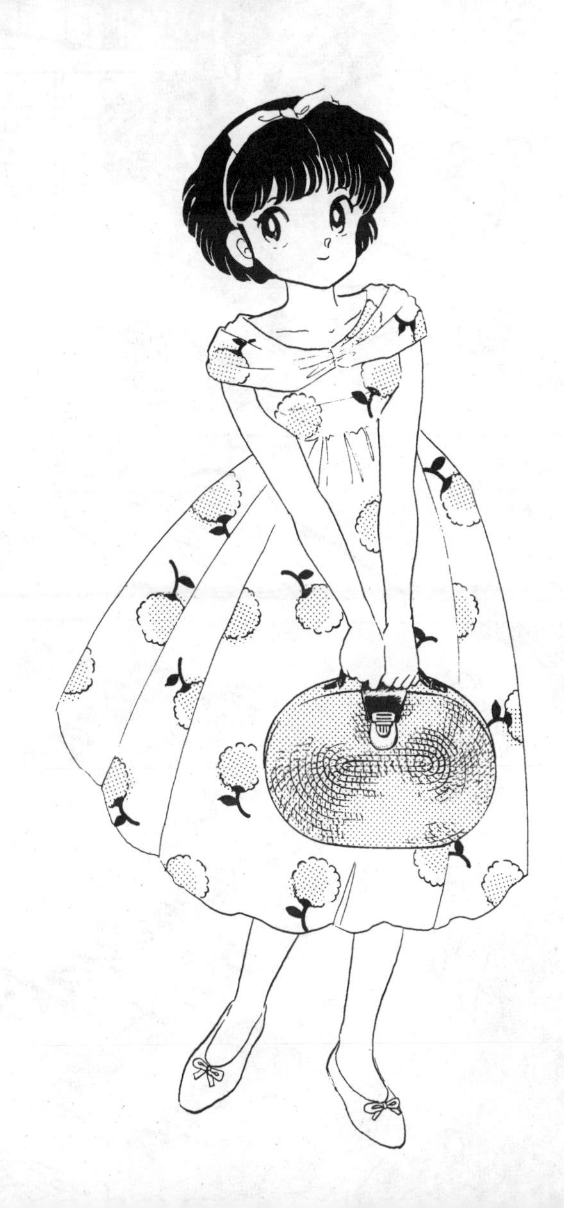

AKANE AND RYOGA ARE GOING TO HAVE A WONDERFUL DATE...
OKONOMIYAKI
Ucchan's
IF I HAVE ANYTHING TO SAY ABOUT IT!
SSSS SSSS
AFTER ALL, IF THEY HIT IT OFF...
...RANMA WILL BELONG TO *ME!*
SPLP

HEH. A LOVE LETTER NO ONE COULD RESIST!
Akane, meet me at Ucchan's Okonomiyaki at 2 pm today --Ryoga
SSSSSS

TENDO TRAINING HALL
天道道場
AKANE! ♪
HM?
THAT VOICE...
A FRIEND OF YOURS, AKANE?
OH, DAD! LET ME INTRODUCE YOU!
SKRATCH SKRATCH
THIS IS RANMA'S CUTE FIANCÉE... UKYO KUONJI.
THE CUTE ONE, IS IT...?
SHIK SHIK
GOOD MORNING AND NICE TO MEET YOU.

YOU GOT ME INTO THIS.
SHK SHK
YOU GOT ME ENGAGED TO THAT STUPID UKYO. SO YOU HANDLE IT!
SHK SHK
ARRGL ARRGL
IF AKANE'S OLD MAN FINDS OUT ABOUT THIS, HE'S GONNA BE PRETTY--
SHK SHK

--ANGRY!!
DOOOOM
PWORK
P-TOO!
CAR

SO.
WHAT DO YOU WANT WITH ME?

BE HONEST, AKANE. THINGS AREN'T GOING WELL WITH YOU AND RAN-CHAN, ARE THEY?
"RAN-CHAN"?

YOU KNOW, RANMA HONEY! YOU DON'T MIND NOT BEING HIS FIANCÉE ANYMORE, DO YOU?
NOW LISTEN...
KLAK

DON'T TELL ME YOU REALLY LOVE EACH OTHER!
.....

NO! HE COULDN'T *POSSIBLY* BE IN LOVE WITH--
VROOOM
HOLD IT, YOU!
VIP
VIP
--WITH A MACHO CHICK LIKE HER? GET REAL!
BAM

THEN YOU'RE *NOT* IN LOVE?
HOW'D YOU GUESS?
PONG

TARAN TA RAAAA
BOP
THIS IS YOUR MESS, IDIOT! FIX IT!
YOU DO REALIZE WHAT WILL HAPPEN...

...IF YOU LEAVE AKANE!
PADOOOOM
COME ON, AKANE! YOU AND I CAN SETTLE THIS!
DON'T LET ME DOWN!

FAP

A NOTE-- ?!

CHOMP

WOP

"MEET ME AT UCCHAN'S AT 2:00 P.M. TODAY."
Ucchan's Okonomiyaki at 2 pm today.
"AKANE...

WAIT A MINUTE... YOU'RE SETTING UP AKANE AND RYOGA FOR A DATE ?!
I JUST GAVE HER THE LOVE-NOTE.
YUP.

A CHALLENGE !
SNARF SNARF SNARF

NO WAY AKANE'S GONNA SHOW!
YOU SOUND AWFULLY SURE OF YOURSELF.

HEH. I GUESS YOU HAVEN'T HEARD...

...THAT AKANE'S THE BIGGEST MACHO DWEEB IN THE HISTORY OF JAPAN!

OH, HE ASKED ME OUT! HE REALLY ASKED ME OUT!
TEE HEE!
GIGGLE
OH, I HOPE I HAVE SOMETHING PRETTY ENOUGH TO WEAR!

IF YOU CAN GET AKANE ACTING LIKE THAT...
heh

...I'LL DRESS UP LIKE A GIRL AND RUN AROUND THE NEIGHBORHOOD A HUNDRED TIMES!
WAHAHAHA
GASP!!

I NEVER DREAMED SUCH AN UNFEMININE GIRL...
...COULD POSSIBLY EXIST...!

OH NO...
THAT CHANGES EVERYTHING...
STAGGER

CAN'T EVEN ASK HER OUT ON HIS OWN!
AND RYOGA...

...IF HE WERE HALF AS MANLY AS AKANE!
HE'D BE TWICE THE MAN HE IS...
BOING BOING

...CAN'T EVEN FIND TOKYO.
Please don't talk to the Horses
ZEEE ZEEE
WHERE IS UCCHAN'S OKONOMIYAKI SHOP?!
MEANWHILE, RYOGA...

CHA-KAASSSHH

HIYAAA!
KDOOM
YOU DON'T MIND NOT BEING HIS FIANCÉE ANYMORE, DO YOU?
YEAH, RIGHT.
SHE SHOWS UP FROM OUT OF NOWHERE, AND--

I'LL BE THERE, UKYO!
WHAK

BUMM

RANMA...
ISN'T IT ALMOST TIME? DON'T YOU HAVE TO GET READY?

I DON'T SEE THAT IT'S ANY BUSINESS OF YOURS, RANMA.

IN FACT, TAKE MY ADVICE... AND STAY OUT OF OUR WAY!
OH, RIGHT, LIKE I'D...

"OUR WAY"?!

NO.
Y-YOU'RE NOT REALLY GOING...?

WHAT ELSE CAN I DO... AFTER A NOTE LIKE THAT?!
GAA!

HEY, S-SINCE WHEN DID YOU TURN INTO A...
THIS IS WHAT I LIVE FOR!
JAB
JAB

AND ONE MORE THING, RANMA...

I DON'T CARE WHO *IS*...OR *ISN'T*... YOUR FIANCÉE.
.....
THAT'S NOT WHY I'M DOING...
HUH?
FOOEY. SO SHE DOESN'T CARE, EH?

BWAHAHAHA!
HOW DO YOU LIKE *THAT*, RANMA!?
JUST STAY OUT OF *OUR* WAY, OKAY?
TEE-HEE!
NO WAY. NO... WAY...

...YOU GET AWAY WITH THIS!
BLOOSH

SLAM
chan's
I'M HERE!
AKANE!
YAKI
OH, I'M SO HAPPY YOU CAME!
OF COURSE I CAME!
THEN THAT MEANS YOU HAVE SOME FEELINGS FOR HIM AFTER ALL!
Heh
HUH?
WHAT ARE YOU TALKING AB--
ZHOOOOOP

I...
I MADE IT...

RUH...
RYOGA...?
FWOMP

UM... THIS IS A DUEL... RIGHT?
WHAT ARE YOU, CRAZY?
VISHH
SHMP

AND HOW MANY WEEKS AGO WAS THAT?
UH... THANKS...?
I BOUGHT THEM AS I LEFT THE HOUSE.
AHEM
WILT

IN HONOR OF YOUR FIRST DATE...
Love
SSSSSSSS

SHE'S TRYING TO SET ME UP WITH HIM...
NOW I GET IT!

SHUDDER
TREMBLE
OUR FIRST... WHAT?
...THIS ONE'S ON ME.

DOES SHE REALLY THINK I'LL FALL FOR THAT?
...SO SHE CAN HAVE RANMA TO HERSELF!

AND HERE'S POOR, GOOD-HEARTED RYOGA, CAUGHT IN HER SCHEME...
PEEK
......

......
AHEM
FIDGET FIDGET
KRAK

IT'S...IT'S GOOD... ISN'T IT? HEE HEE HEE HEE HEE HEE HEE!
SNARF SNARF SNARF
WAHA HAHA HAHA HA!

SO THEY THINK THEY'RE GONNA HAVE A DATE, EH?! NOT WHEN I GET THROUGH WITH 'EM!
Salon 3F
NYAHA HAHA HAHA HA!
SHOOM

PART 6
RYOGA'S WHAT?!

OKONOMIYAKI
Ucchan's
PARTY
OKAY!
PRIVATE PARTY
YOU KIDS BE GOOD WHILE I'M GONE!
HIROSHIMA-STYLE SPECIAL ¥500
HEY!
HUH?
BOING

B-BUT YOU CAN'T JUST LEAVE ME!
I'M GIVING YOU TWO A CHANCE TO BE ALONE.

WHERE DO YOU THINK YOU'RE GOING?!
HM?
ZZZIP

CHMP CHMP
CHMP CHMP
BUT I DON'T KNOW WHAT TO DO!
THIS IS A DATE, FOOL!
PSS PSS PSS PSS

OHHHH... I SEE IT NOW...
UKYO TALKED HIM INTO THIS...HE REALLY DOESN'T WANT TO BE HERE...

IF YOU LIKE HER, STUPID, JUST TELL HER!
PSS PSS PSS PSS
HOW CAN I DO THAT IF I DON'T KNOW IF SHE LIKES ME BACK?!

IF RYOGA DOESN'T WANT TO DATE ME, YOU CAN'T FORCE HIM TO...

W-WAIT! STOP!
OH PLEASE DON'T LEAVE ME! PLEASE! PLEASE! PLEASE!
AAARGH!
ARE YOU A MAN OR AREN'T YOU?!
BONK
BONK

GLARE

HE DOES WANT TO!
I DO WANT TO!
HUF HUF
HUF
IN FACT, I'VE ALWAYS BEEN IN... IN...
IN WHAT? IN WHAT?!
TONK
YOU TWO-TIMER!!
BOOM
WHA...?
TOOM TOOM
HOW DARE YOU GO OUT WITH HER...

...WHEN YOU HAVE ME!
GOON
YOU?!

HEH! WHAT A DISGUISE!

I'M INNOCENT, I TELL YOU, INNOCENT! I NEVER SAW HER BEFORE!

FLAP FLAP

JUST WHO ARE YOU?
POO.
WHO AM I?

hmm m...
GASP

I...AM RYOGA'S...
FIANCÉE!
GASP

HWOOOO
FIANCÉE ?!
DOOOOM
KLANG KLANG KLANG
H-HOW COULD I NOT KNOW...
...THAT I HAD A FIANCÉE?!
YOU SEE...
IT'S NOT YOUR FAULT YOU DON'T KNOW.

...WE WERE BUT BABES WHEN OUR PARENTS ARRANGED OUR UNION!
TWONK
.....

WHY DID YOU DO THAT, YOU VIOLENT GIRL YOU!
GRRRR!
JUST WHAT DO YOU THINK YOU'RE DOING?
KLANG KLANG KLANG
WHAT AM I GOING TO DOOOO...?
WOK
DON'T JUST SIT THERE!

ARE YOU GOING TO LET SOME GIRL COME OUT OF NOWHERE AND CLAIM YOUR FIANCÉE?!
OH!

NO...I WILL HESITATE NO LONGER!

BOOM
I'M IN LOVE WITH AKANE!

WHA...
?
AKANE
!!
VIP

I AM
IN L--

?
WH-WHAT
ARE YOU
DOING?!
BA-BUMP
BA-BUMP
SPLOOSH

IF YOU
TRY TO
LEAVE
ME...

GYAAH! CUT IT OUT!
...I'LL DO THIS!!
SHOOM SHOOM
KLATTER
SPLISH
SPLASH
UM...
SHK SHK
THAT LITTLE... AND JUST WHEN AKANE AND RYOGA WERE ABOUT TO GET TOGETHER, TOO! WELL...
H-HEY, LEGGO!
OH, RYOGA, WE MUST ESCAPE THOSE WHO ENVY OUR LOVE!
CLOMP
VRRRMMMM
TONNG
WHOA!
SHA
...JUST LET HER TRY!
SHA

YOU... YOU...
YOU WON'T GET AWAY!!
.....
KEEP OFF GRASS

WAIT. WHY AM I HIDING?! I DIDN'T...
SHH!
LISTEN, I ALREADY HAVE A GIRL I'M IN--
I KNOW THAT... P-CHAN.
TWING

I'M YOUR FIANCÉE!
MAN, THIS IS FUN!

WHAT A MAROON! HE STILL HASN'T FIGURED THIS OUT!
H-H-HOW DO YOU KN-KN-KNOW ABOUT...?

BLUSH
SHOULDN'T I KNOW EVERYTHING ABOUT THE MAN I'LL MARRY?

WOBBLE
SHE... SHE KNOWS! AND YET...

SIGH
...YOU STILL WANT ME?!
WHA-- ?!

YOU'VE MADE ME...SO HAPPY!
PAK
WHOA! WHOA! DON'T GET WEIRD ON ME!

AAAARGH!
...THE GIRL I'M GOING TO MARRY!
GOOSH

WHY YOU'RE...
WHO DO YOU THINK I AM?!

HM?
FLAPPA
GET OFFA ME, YOU PERVERT!!
BIFF BAM POW

ZEE ZEE
JEEZ... THAT WAS CLOSE!

POOM
RYOGA!
YOU DON'T DESERVE TO BE MIXED UP IN THIS.
POOR RYOGA...

OH...!

IS THERE SOME *REASON* YOU HATE RYOGA?
KLOK

GWAAAA!

SORRY YOUR DATE DIDN'T WORK OUT. HEH.
WH... ?
KEEP OFF GRASS

IT... CAN'T BE.

RANMA... WERE YOU JEALOUS ?!

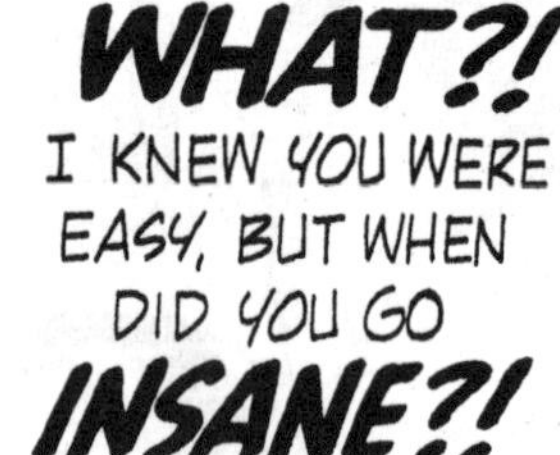
WHAT?! I KNEW YOU WERE EASY, BUT WHEN DID YOU GO INSANE?!

"EASY"... ?
RUSHING OFF TO SEE RYOGA JUST 'CAUSE HE DRIBBLED YOU A LOVE LETTER IN SAUCE?

AND WHO ARE YOU TO TALK...
BLORBLE

...YOU PERVERT ?!
OUCH!
BOOT

A DATE...
I THOUGHT IT WAS A DUEL!

IF THAT'S THE WAY YOU SEE ME...
WELL, FINE!

ICE CREAM
GIGGLE GIGGLE
TEE HEE
SHFF SHFF
......
PLEASE PUT TRASH WHERE IT

SHE COULDN'T JUST BOOT ME, SHE HAD TO SPLASH ME FIRST.
STUPID... MACHO... DWEEB!
SHFF

...THEY'D THINK I WAS SOME KINDA PERVERT!

IF ANYBODY SAW ME, DRESSED AS AS A GIRL...
BOOF

GASP!

PERVERT! GET HIM!!
NO! WAIT! STOP!
EH?
WHAK
BOOM
POW
BAM

PEEK

RAN-CHAN!

WHAT WERE YOU DOING THERE?
JJJJJ
STUPID... AKANE...!

STUPID RANMA!
JUST FOR THAT, I WILL DATE RYOGA!
JJJJJJ

PART 7
AT LONG LAST...THE DATE!

THEY SEEM TO BE HITTING IT OFF TOO.
AKANE'S REALLY ON A DATE WITH RYOGA?
OH MY!
TENDO TRAINING HALL
天道道場

NO WAY.
WA-HA-HA.
RANMA, DON'T YOU THINK YOU SHOULD GO CHECK ON HER?

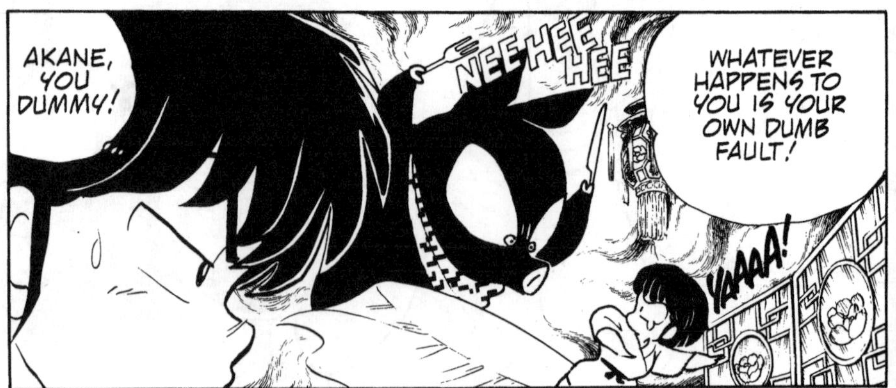
WHATEVER HAPPENS TO YOU IS YOUR OWN DUMB FAULT!
NEEHEE HEE
AKANE, YOU DUMMY!
YAAAA!

SHE'LL BE FINE. SHE'S STRONG AS A BULL.
FEH
SERIOUSLY, RANMA... WHY DON'T YOU GO AND GET AKANE?
RAAAAAN-MAAAAA!
OOOWOOOOO
RANMA... I REALLY THINK YOU SHOULD GO.
UH... YEAH...

GET REAL!
THEN YOU'LL RESCUE HER IF SHE'S IN TROUBLE, RAN-CHAN?
REALTY
Beauty Salon
UGS
CAFE Rendezvous
I'M SORRY, RYOGA.
WUH...?
I HOPE IT'S NOT TOO MUCH TROUBLE FOR YOU!
MAKING YOU COME WITH ME LIKE THIS...

TH-THIS HAS TO BE...
A DREAM!

AKANE ASKING ME OUT LIKE THIS...
...IT CAN'T REALLY BE HAPPENING!

I'LL AWAKEN AND IT WILL ALL BE GONE!
HEY! NO HEADBANGING ALLOWED!
BONG
BONG
BONG
SPOOT

KRIKKLE
TAKTAK

IT DIDN'T HURT... IT IS A DREAM.
SOB

KONG
RUN!

POINK
R...RYOGA...?

THAT HURT...
...A LITTLE...

IT'S NOT A DREAM!
WHY DON'T WE...GO SOMEWHERE ELSE?

THEY SEEM TO BE HAVING FUN.
RRUMBLE
POP
HMPH

TWEET
TWEET

COME ON, LET'S RENT A BOAT!
HEY!
BOAT RENTALS
ERK
BE AWFUL IF YOU FELL IN, WOULDN'T IT... P-CHAN?
POIK
BOOM

.....
QUIT FOLLOWING US AROUND!
DON'T YOU MIND US NOW!
NO FISHING
16
RANMA AND I ARE ON OUR OWN DATE.
OH?
SO FIRST HE TRIES TO KEEP RYOGA AND ME APART...
WHOOM
...THEN HE TURNS AROUND AND ASKS YOU OUT, EH?!
WHOA.
NO FISHING
11
SPLAT

YOU TWO-TIMER. YOU'VE LOST ALL RIGHT TO CALL YOURSELF AKANE'S FIANCÉ!
RAN-CHAN!
BLOOSH
BLBLBLBL...
OOF!
EEK!
WHO IS A TWO-TIMER... RYOGA?!

SKWEEEEE
.....
HOW DARE YOU DO THIS WHEN YOU HAVE ME?!
WHA?
WHA?
WHA?
HUH HUH HUH
WHEN YOU JUMPED ALL OVER ME...

...WAS THAT JUST A LARK?!
WAP WAP WAP
I WAS... I WAS...
SKRITCH SKRITCH

SHE KNOWS... BUT STILL LOVES ME!
HOW CAN I EVER HOPE TO FIND ANOTHER GIRL WHO'LL... WHO'LL...
WELL, I STILL WANT YOU... EVEN IF YOU'RE A PIG!
SOBB

HOW MANY TIMES DO YOU HAVE TO GET IN THE WAY, GIRL?!
WOOSH
YOW!
DUCK

YOU'RE THE ONLY ONE FOR ME!
SKWISH
ARE YOU SURE YOU'RE SURE?!

I THINK YOU SHOULD RUN, RANMA.
WHAT? WHO'S RANMA?

IT'S... YOU...!
HM?

C'MON, RYOGA! CANTCHA TAKE A JOKE?
RANMA...?
KRAK KRAK
RAAAAN-MAAA!
WHOA!
JAB
YOU WILL DIE!!

MORON.
AK!
KWEE KWEE

COMP

I WILL NOT...
PLOOSH

...GET WET!
KONK

BLURRRBLE
BOING
BOING
EEEEEEK!
FRUIT TIME

TAP
HWOOOOO
.....

NO MATTER THE CAUSE...FOR A BRIEF MOMENT, MY HEART BETRAYED AKANE...

RANMA, YOU'RE SUCH A JERK!
KWEEEEE
DO YOU HAVE *FUN* TORMENTING RYOGA?
SPLAT
I'M SO SORRY, RYOGA.
RANMA'S SUCH A...
AKANE...
GOODBYE.
I CAN SEE YOU...NO MORE.

WHAT...?

RYOGA! WAIT--!
DASH

I NO LONGER HAVE THE RIGHT TO LOVE YOU, AKANE!

RYOGA!
VOOM
IT'S ALL YOUR FAULT, RANMA!

I DIDN'T THINK IT'D HURT HIM THIS MUCH!

HHSSSHHHH H H
Sprinkler in Use *

OH...
......

P-CHAN...?
WHY ARE YOU H--

P-CHAN!
WAIT!
DASH

PLEASE, P-CHAN.
SCREECH

NEEE?

COME HERE.
VOOOM

DO YOU THINK RYOGA'S GONE FOR GOOD?
OH, I HOPE NOT, RYOGA!
BWEE!
GREAT SET OF ROMANTIC PRINCIPLES YOU GOT THERE, PIG.

RANMA, YOU BE SURE TO APOLOGIZE WHEN RYOGA COMES BACK.
I THINK HE'S ALREADY GOTTEN OVER IT.
THIS IS FUN NO MATTER HOW MANY TIMES I DO IT!
BLUB BLUB BLUB
BITE BITE BITE BITE BITE BITE

PART 8
HAPPOSAI DAYS ARE HERE AGAIN

HHHSSSS
EEEEEK! BIKINI THIEF!

MM?

SHHHH

GIVE IT BACK!
YOU PERVERT!
EEEEE
EEEE
EEEEE
VRROOMM
SNAK SHACK

YOU SENILE DELINQUENT!
WHOMP
FOOEY. WELL, IF I CAN'T GO TREASURE HUNTING, I'M GOING GIRL-HUNTING!
HHSSSH

FWOK
WHERE DO YOU THINK?
WHERE DO YOU GET YOUR ENERGY?
PRETTY LADIES!
EEEEEEE
EEEEEEEEE
WANTA EAT SOME WATERMELON ?!
EEEEEEEE
BRIGHT SUN!
WHITE CLOUDS!
BLUE SKIES!
GYAAAAAAH!
GROPE GROPE
AAAH! I FEEL SO YOUNG!
GROPE GROPE
IF YOU'RE LOOKING FOR THE CLOUDS, THEY'RE BEHIND YOU.
I LOVE THE SEA!
SIGH

BOOOT
THERE MUST BE SOME WAY TO CALM HIM DOWN...
HUF HUF
BOY
CAT CAFE
AIYAAA!
NIHAO, RANMA!
VACANCY
SHAMPOO...
CHILLED RAMEN!? OVER HERE!
BOY
CAT CAFE

WHAT ARE YOU TWO GIRLS DOING?!
IT'S A COINCIDENCE!
GOOSH
PRR PRR PRR
I SO HAPPY! RANMA COME TO BEACH AFTER SHAMPOO!

DATE HUH?
I GOT IT!

RANMA, YOU DATE WITH SHAMPOO AFTER WORK?
OH, SO YOU DO BUSINESS ON THE BEACH DURING SUMMER...

YOU'LL INTRODUCE ME TO A G-GIRL?!
SAY WHAT?!
INN

IT'S TRUE! SO LAY OFF THE BIKINI STEALING FOR A WHILE!
IT'S TOO GOOD TO BE TRUE!
point

DUMP
LUCKY I BROUGHT MY TREASURE CHEST ALONG!
NO TOUCH
MY PRECIOUS

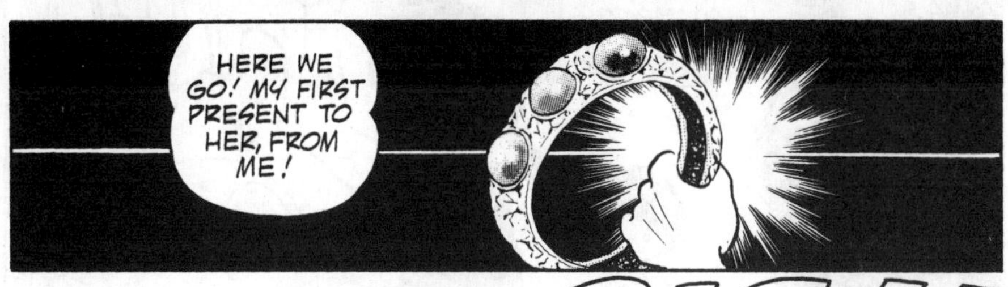
HERE WE GO! MY FIRST PRESENT TO HER, FROM ME!

LISTEN, RANMA, MY TYPE HAS LONG HAIR AND BIG EYES...
YEP, THAT SOUNDS JUST LIKE HER.

SIGH

RANMA! YOU'RE NOT GOING TO INTRODUCE HIM TO SHAMPOO!?

SHE'LL TURN HIM DOWN FLAT!
YOU THINK SO?
FLAP FLAP
CAT CAFE
PUBLIC SHOWERS
CHINESE NOODLES
SODA
RANMA!
YO, SHAMPOO.
BLUSH
point
OH, WHAT A WIFE SHE'LL MAKE...
GETTING A FEW STEPS AHEAD OF YOURSELF, AREN'T YOU?
POIK
I'D LIKE TO INTRODUCE A FRIEND OF MINE...
RAMEN 500
RAMUNE 200
ICE 150
point

THERE. DO I DELIVER, OR WHAT?
HE SAY HE WANT DATE WITH YOU, GREAT-GRANDMOTHER.
OH YEAH?

TEARS OF HAPPINESS, OLD MAN?
WHO IS THIS OLD FREAK?
BOO HOO HOO HOO HOO HOO

LONG HAIR!
BRRR BRRR BRRR
BIG EYES!

IS GOOD COUPLE.
OF COURSE! SHAMPOO'S GREAT-GRANDMOTHER IS THE PERFECT AGE FOR HIM!

LET'S LEAVE THESE LOVEBIRDS ALONE.
AND WE KIDS GO PLAY!
STOP!

THIS IS FOR A DOWRY.
BOING
AIYAA, IS BEAUTIFUL BRACELET!

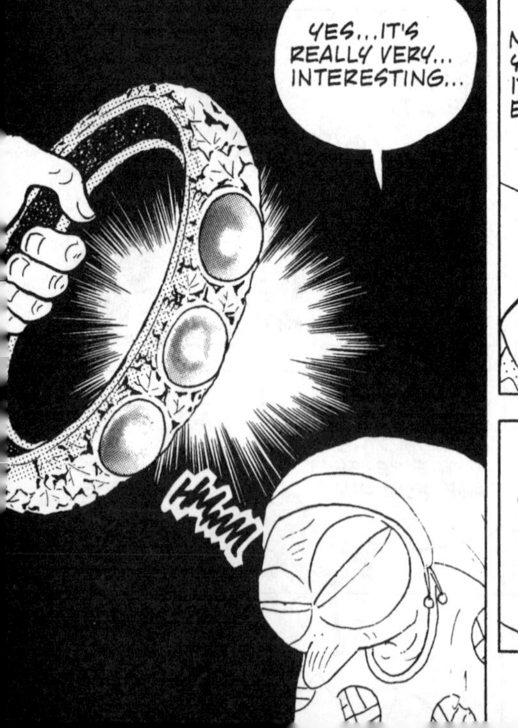

YES...IT'S REALLY VERY... INTERESTING...

NOW THAT YOU MENTION IT, IT LOOKS EXPENSIVE.
DID YOU STEAL IT?
HOW DARE YOU!

THIS IS A MEMENTO OF MY FIRST LOVE.
SIGH
OH...?

WHEN I WAS EIGHTEEN...
Once upon a time in China.
...AS A PART OF MY TRAINING, I TRAVELLED TO CHINA. AND THERE...

...I MET A BEAUTIFUL VILLAGE GIRL WHO STOLE MY HEART!
Happosai, age 18
OH, GIVE ME A BREAK!

A MAN IN TRAINING CANNOT AFFORD LOVE! FAREWELL!
OH, WHAT TRAGEDY!

WOOSH
PLEASE, TAKE THIS TO REMEMBER ME!

YES, YES...
...A TRAGIC STORY, INDEED...
THAT WAS THE LAST I SAW OF HER...

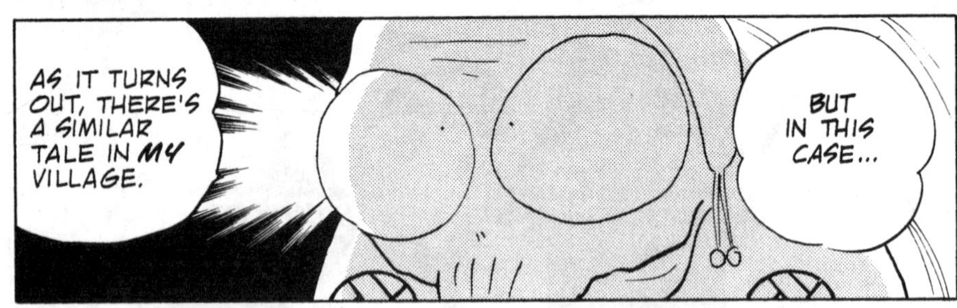
BUT IN THIS CASE...
AS IT TURNS OUT, THERE'S A SIMILAR TALE IN MY VILLAGE.

...AND GOT TURNED DOWN BY ALL OF THEM...
THE MAN HIT ON EVERY GIRL IN THE VILLAGE...
EEK
EEK
EEK

TSK TSK.
WHAT A HORRIBLE MAN.
...SO HE STOLE ALL OUR VALUABLES AND RAN AWAY!
GET 'IM!
GET 'IM!

HWOOO
SQUINT
WELL, YOU OUGHT TO KNOW...
...YOU CRIMINAL!
VOOOM
HO!

SSSSS SSSSS
OH! OH!
TOP

LIFE'S JUST FULL OF SURPRISES.
MAYBE INTRODUCING THEM WAS A BAD IDEA.

WHAT?
YOU WILL RETURN THAT FAMILY HEIRLOOM.

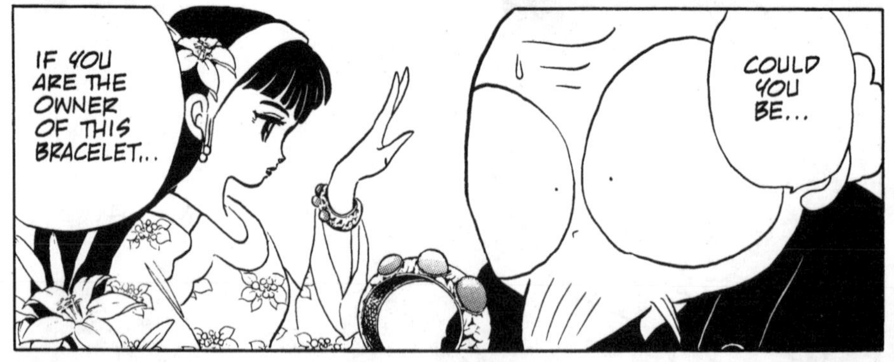
COULD YOU BE...
IF YOU ARE THE OWNER OF THIS BRACELET...

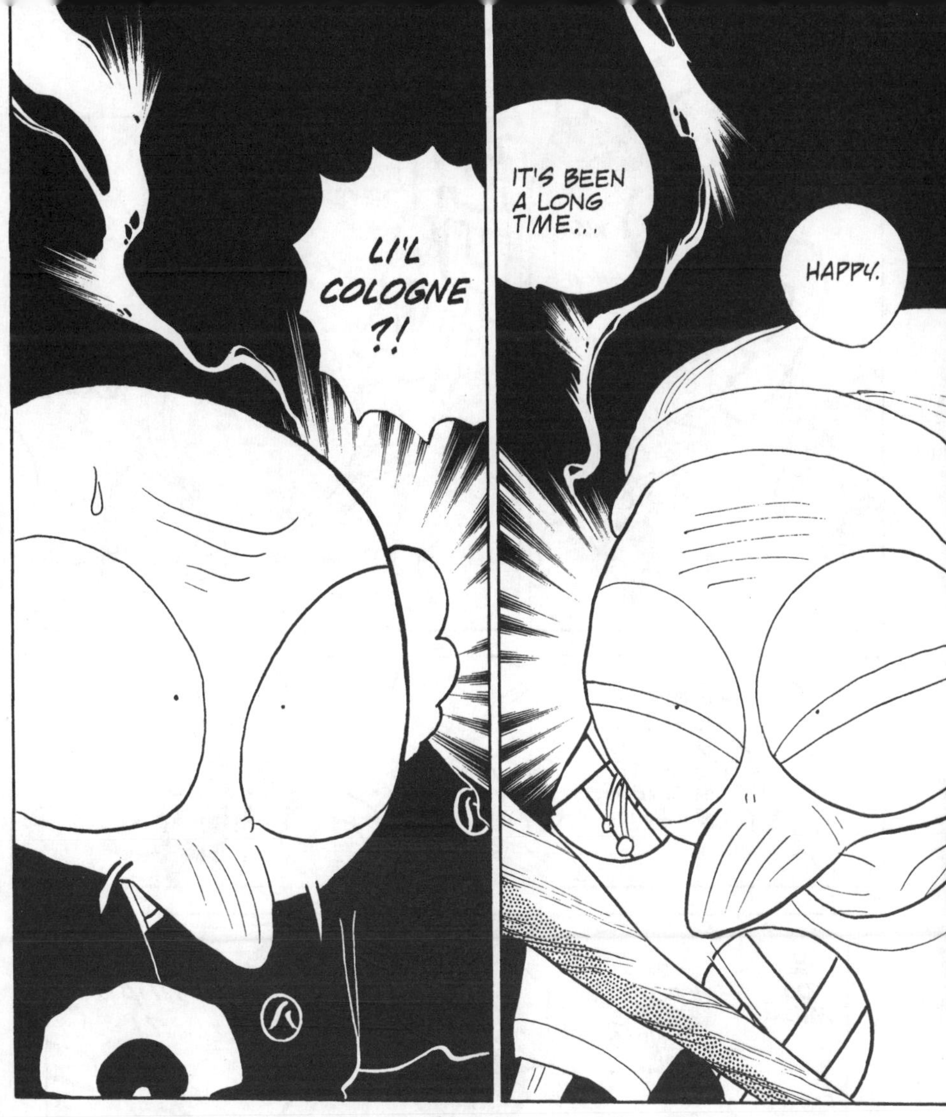
IT'S BEEN A LONG TIME...
HAPPY.
LI'L COLOGNE ?!

IF YOU KNOW THE NICKNAME I WAS CALLED IN MY YOUTH... THEN YOU ARE COLOGNE...
IS SHORT FOR "HAPPOSAI," YES?
"COLOGNE" ?!
"HAPPY" ?!

POOF
FAREWELL YOUTH!
WAH! A SMOKE SCREEN!
WA HA HA HA HA
NOW THAT I KNOW IT'S AN HEIRLOOM--I'LL NEVER RETURN IT!
YOU... YOU... MONSTER!

SHAMPOO, YOU MUST GET THAT BRACELET BACK BEFORE HE DISCOVERS ITS SECRET!
SECRET...?

IF YOU FAIL...
...THIS WORLD WILL BECOME A LIVING HELL!
WHAT?!
BRR BRR BRR

PART 9
ONE MOMENT TO LOVE

SO THE SECRET OF THE BRACELET...
HISSSHHHH!

...IS ITS LOVE PILLS?
CORRECT.
SHKK
SHKK
SHKK

THERE ARE PILLS IMBEDDED IN THAT BRACELET...
...MAKE THE SWALLOWER FALL IN LOVE WITH THE FIRST PERSON OF THE OPPOSITE SEX HE OR SHE SEES!
WHOO...
HOW TERRIFYING...
SHKK
SHKK
SHKK
...WHICH, IF SWALLOWED...
...THEN IT REALLY WILL BE HELL ON EARTH!
IF HAPPY DISCOVERS THOSE PILLS...
NYEH HEHE HEH!
FLAP FLAP

SPOING
NYEHEHEH!
I HEARD YOU, I HEARD YOU!
CURSE YOU, HAPPY!
SHAVED ICE

OH, SHAMPOO, BABY!
NIHAO!

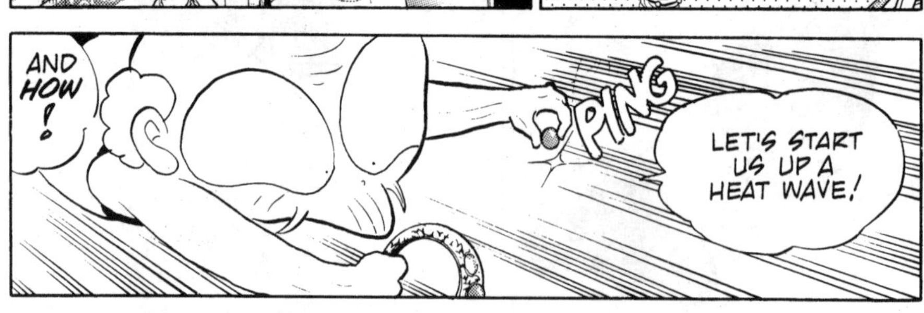

AND HOW!
PING
LET'S START US UP A HEAT WAVE!

AAAAAAH...

SPLAT
VIP

NO!! IT'S A TRAP!!
SCHILL

I GOT YOU NOW, FREAK!

WHOP
HOI!
WAHAHAHA
HE GOT AWAY!

HOW DARE YOU TREAT YOUR MASTER SO!
KLONG

SO THAT'S THE FAMOUS LOVE PILL, EH...?
BUT HE DROP ONE.

LET SEE IF PILL REALLY WORK.
POP

......
WHOMPF

NO GET IN WAY!
OH? DID I GET IN YOUR WAY?

HM?

MAN... YOU'RE CUTE!
HUH?

...MAKE THE SWALLOWER FALL IN LOVE WITH THE FIRST PERSON OF THE OPPOSITE SEX HE OR SHE SEES!

N-NO... WAIT...
BLUSH!
I MEAN WAY CUTE!

ONLY KIDDING!
MWAAAH!

TH-THAT'S THE LOVE PILL TALKING, IT'S NOT REALLY--
NOT LIKE THIS!
FLUTTER FLUTTER

WHSH WHSH
BWAHAHAHAHAHA!
YOU FELL FOR IT, YOU DUMMY!

WHAP
How's it going, son?
GLMP!

YOU THINK I'D ACTUALLY SWALLOW THIS THING ?!

LOOK... WHAT YOU MADE ME DO...!
WOBBLE
SHOWERS
LOC
SOB
VROOM
RANMA, YOU LOOK SHAMPOO!
OH NO, YOU DON'T!
YOU OLD GHOUL!
JERK
YOU'VE GOT TO HAVE AN ANTI... ANTI...

GASP

HOW... HOW COULD I...
HOW COULD I NEVER SEE...
point
...JUST HOW *LOVELY* A WOMAN IN FULL BLOOM CAN BE!?
OH, YOU DON'T MEAN IT!
GLOMP
GASP! OH MY GAWD
GREAT-GRANDMOTHER, NO FAIR!

YOU STAY AWAY!
HYAH
NEVER!
ZIP
NO ONE WILL EVER COME BETWEEN US!

NOW, COLOGNE!
VOOM
YOU MUST MARRY ME! NOW!
RANMA!

RANMA SERIOUS!
N-NO!

NOOOO!
RANMA, DON'T GO!

HOLD IT RIGHT THERE, SON!
BOOT

I OPPOSE THIS MARRIAGE!
melon
GLUK
HUH...?

WHAT ARE YOU TALKING ABOUT?
BLINK

EH?
RANMA?

TO MARRY THAT WOMAN, YOU MUST DEFEAT ME FIRST!
JUST WHO DO YOU THINK I'M TRYING TO MARRY?!

ME, DEARIE.

PILL WEAR OFF?
YES.

WHAT OUR LITTLE... GROOM... SWALLOWED WAS THE "INSTANT" PILL.
INSTANT PILL?

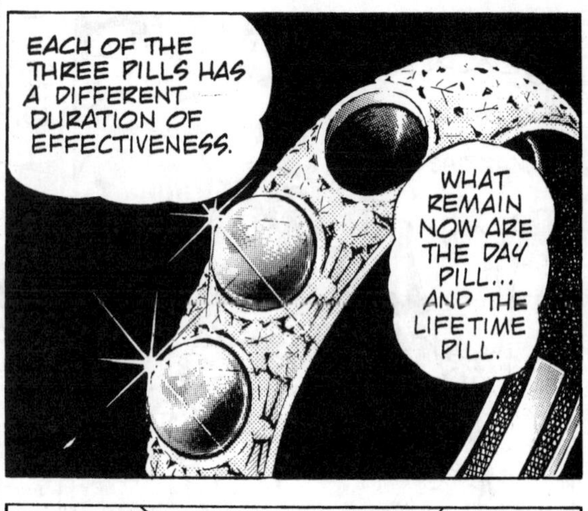
EACH OF THE THREE PILLS HAS A DIFFERENT DURATION OF EFFECTIVENESS.
WHAT REMAIN NOW ARE THE DAY PILL... AND THE LIFETIME PILL.

THE DAY PILL'S EFFECTS LAST ONE ENTIRE DAY...
THEN THE LIFETIME PILL LASTS...?

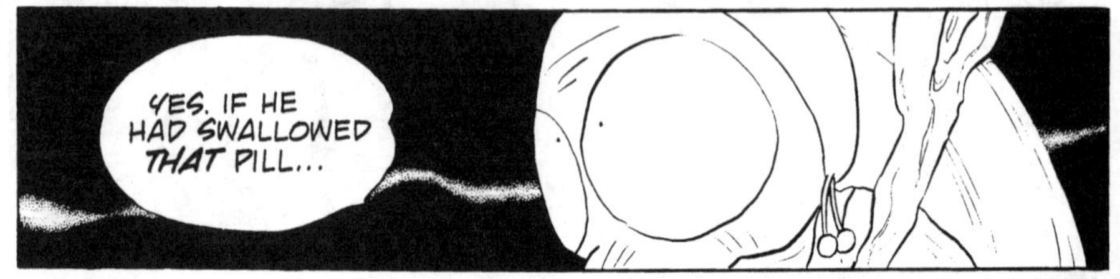
YES. IF HE HAD SWALLOWED THAT PILL...

I'D BE SENDING OUT INVITATIONS TO OUR WEDDING!
NYAHAHAHA!
THAT WAS CLOSE ONE, RANMA.
I DON'T THINK HE HEARS YOU...

BOOOOOM
TEE HEE HEE
WHEEE!

BABUMP BABUMP
NOW WHICH GIRL SHALL I PICK?

HYOI
HAPPY?

YOU DATE WITH SHAMPOO?

TOP
OH SHAMPOO! ♪

CHIRRUP CHEEERUP RUP-RUP
HONESTLY, RANMA.
INN
OOOHHH OOOHHHH
BOO HOO HOO
JUST GET OVER IT, WILL YOU?

TUP
IS PERFECT.
SHAMPOO?
THAT BRACELET...!
SHAMPOO... HOW COULD YOU?
BOO HOO HOO

I MAKE RANMA TAKE THIS WHILE HE SLEEP!
POP

DON'T YOU EVER GIVE UP?!
WHSHHH

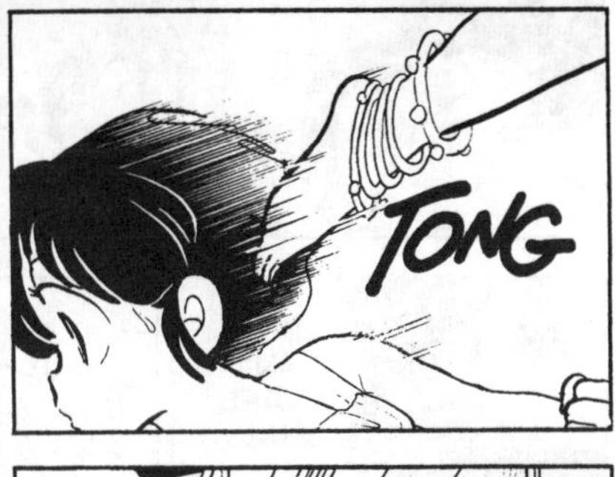
TONG

AAAKK!
FLAP FLAP

NOW, RANMA...
YOU FALL IN LOVE WITH SHAMPOO!
SNAG
NGAAA

ERG!
BOING

HOW DO YOU LIKE THIS ?!
BLOOSH
BWAH!
IT DOESN'T WORK WHEN YOU'RE BOTH GIRLS!
WH-WHAT THE-- ?

FEH...
AFTER RANMA TAKE PILL...
FLIP
...I CHANGE RANMA BACK!
VIP
POIK
OW!
HAHAHA! YOU MISS--
--ED!
POP

GLMP
AIYAAA!
UH-OH!

PART 10
I WON'T FALL IN LOVE!

WHAT?! A LOVE PILL?! AKANE?!
CHIRRUP
CHIRRUP-RUP-RUP
INN

TWEEE TWEEE
THAT MEANS... THE FIRST MAN SHE SEES...
...SHE'LL FALL IN LOVE WITH.
BURBLE URBLE
HOT HOT HOT HOT!
NOW AKANE-- LOOK AT RANMA!
SHOVE
VSSH!

I NO THINK SO!
BOING
SPLASH
BWAH!

DAD! WILL YOU STOP INTERFERING ?!
BUT AKANE...

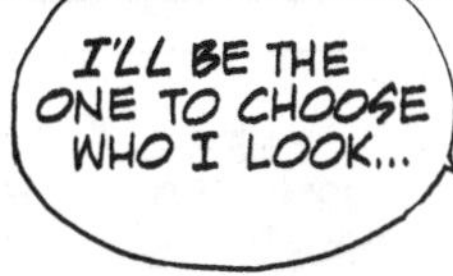
I'LL BE THE ONE TO CHOOSE WHO I LOOK...

OH AKANE--! ♪
POP

KABOOOM
INN

TWINK!
THE ONLY PILLS LEFT WERE...

THE DAY PILL AND THE LIFETIME PILL. WHICH ONE DID YOU SWALLOW?
I DON'T KNOW...

WHAT HAPPENS IF SHE TOOK THE LIFETIME PILL?
POP
THE EFFECT WOULD LAST HER ENTIRE...

BIFF
BOOM
BAM
No peeking

HHSSSHHHH

ouvenirs
FLAP FLAP
TANNING OIL
CHILLED RAMEN
CAT CAFE
EH...?
COTS FOOD SHOWER

WHICH MEANS ?
NO NEED TO WORRY.
SHKK SHKK

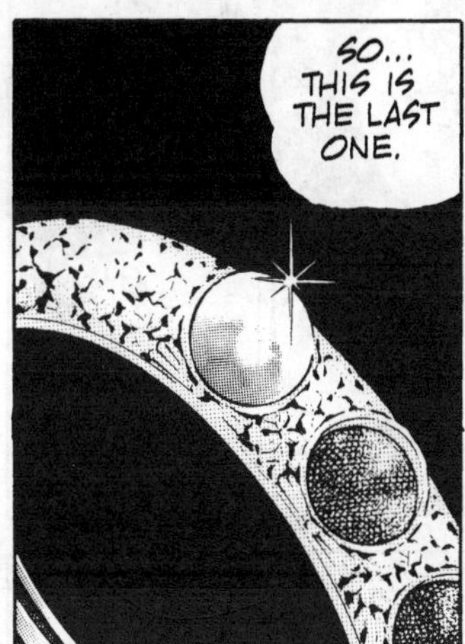

SO... THIS IS THE LAST ONE.

IS THAT ALL ?
REALLY ?!
WHAT YOU SWALLOWED WAS THE DAY PILL.
Phew
CHILLED RAMEN

IF IT'S ONLY THE DAY PILL, WHAT'S THERE TO GET ALL WORKED UP ABOUT?
WHAT D'YOU MEAN, "IS THAT ALL"?

JUST BECAUSE IT'S NOT YOUR PROBLEM...
TAPTAP
......

HM?
No peeking
BEFORE YOU LOOK AT SOMETHING YOU DON'T WANT TO...
SHIMMEER

HOW ABOUT YOU SETTLE FOR ME?

WHA...?

R-REALLY?
OF COURSE NOT, DUMMY!

PFOO!
TUG!
CHILLED RAMEN
MOOSH

ALL I HAVE TO DO IS NOT LOOK AT ANY MEN FOR 24 HOURS!
I'M NOT GOING TO LET SOME PILL BEAT ME!

AKANE!
TMP TMP

LEAVE ME ALONE!

BONG
OKAY. BUT WATCH OUT FOR THAT WALL.

WAHAHAHA
YOU GO, GIRL!
OH SHUT UP!
OBBLE

WHOOPS! SILLY ME! SHE DID SWALLOW THE LIFETIME PILL!

N...NOW WHERE AM I...?
HUF HUF
FOOD
IRS
ICE

I...I CAN'T...
...GO ON...

AKANE... IF YOU ONLY KNEW...

TMP TMP
SQUISH

UH...?
SQUORSH

RANMA, YOU JERK!
BOOOOM
A TINY BIT OF SYMPATHY WOULDN'T KILL YOU!

I'VE HAD ENOUGH!
SO WHAT IF I...
TUG

AKANE!
HM?
TM
TM
TM

VWIP

AKA--
BOOT
......

AKANE, THE PILL YOU SWALLOWED...
P-CHAN, HOW DID YOU...?
THERE'S A PIG DROWNING!
HUF HUF
BU-KEEE!
WHAT WAS THAT FOR!?
KABOOOOM
K-KUNO?!
HIYAAAA! HIYAAAA! HIYAAAA!
ONE HUNDRED SWINGS!
point
point

POOM

HUF HUF HUF HUF
VORP
......

YOU REALLY ARE JEALOUS!
DENY IT ALL YOU WANT, RANMA...

THE PILL YOU SWALLOWED...
LISTEN, AKANE!

WHY ARE YOU SO INTERESTED, HUH?!
LISTEN TO ME!

NYAAAAH!
VROOOOOM
HEY HEY!

MY KNIGHT ON A WHITE HORSE MIGHT COME ALONG!
NO WAY!
PUT ON YOUR BLINDFOLD! IF YOU LOOK AT SOME STRANGE GUY...
HUH?
K-K-KLUMP K-K-KLUMP K-K-KLUMP
WHINNNNEEE
AKANE! ♪
WHAT--?
IS MORE LIKE NUT ON WHITE HORSE.
ACK!

SHFF
HYAAH
GLOMP
DON'T LOOK, AKANE!
EEEK!

BUBBLE URBBLE
URBLE
THWOP
I'LL RESCUE YOU, AKANE!
RANMA, YOU TURN BACK TO BOY-TYPE AND FALL IN LOVE WITH SHAMPOO!
......
HAK HAK HAK HAK-
WAAAH!
B-KEEEE!

......
YOU BETTER APPRECIATE THIS, AKANE!
SOB
SOB
SOB
IF YOU LOOK AT THAT OLD FREAK...
BLORSH
YOUR WHOLE LIFE IS RUINED! SO...

...I'M CHANGING BACK INTO A GUY FOR YOU!
SOB

......
......
YAAWN!

UM...
HAVE YOU... FALLEN FOR ME?

RANMA...

...HOW STUPID WILL YOU GET BEFORE YOU STOP?!

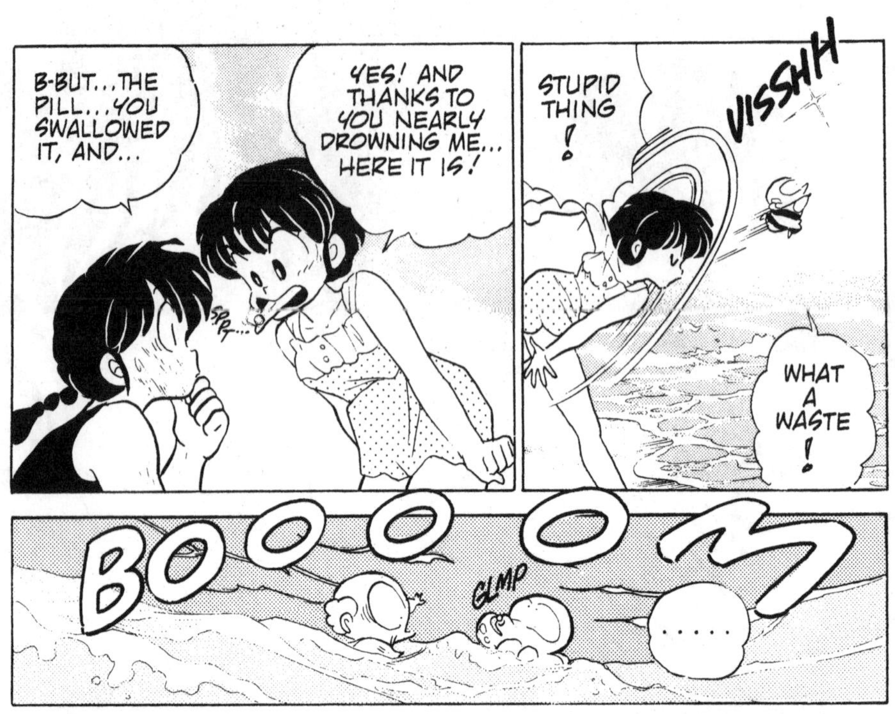
B-BUT...THE PILL...YOU SWALLOWED IT, AND...
YES! AND THANKS TO YOU NEARLY DROWNING ME... HERE IT IS!
STUPID THING!
VISSHH
WHAT A WASTE!
BOOOOM
GLMP
.....

I WAS TRYING TO TELL YOU THAT YOU TOOK THE LIFETIME PILL!
RANMA, YOU TAKE DAY PILL, YES?
OH MY. IS THAT YOUR NEW GIRLFRIEND?
I DID NOT!
BUT I'M NOT AN OCTOPUS!
SOB SOB SOB
THAT'S WHAT YOU SAY!

PART 11
ABDUCTION OF...AKANE?

KARA KARA KARA
TONK
LOTTERY
YOU'RE A WINNER! FOURTH PRIZE!
TINGA LING!
YAAAAAY!
SHOPPING

I'M HAPPY FOR YOU, AKANE.
I'VE BEEN WANTING THIS!
OINK
HEH HEH HEH HEH HEH
AKANE TENDO... BETROTHED OF RANMA SAOTOME...
HUH?

WHO'S THERE !?
HEH
HEH
HEH
HEH
HEH
NOW YOU WILL BE MY HOSTAGE !

OH!!
GLINT

OH MY!
LOOK OUT!
SHH SHH
SHH SHH
THOK

SKWEE
SHP
SKNRK
OINK...
NOW I'VE GOT YOU...
HEH HEH HEH HEH HEH
AND JUST WHO ARE YOU?!
OINK
OH, WHAT A STRANGE MAN.

SHHHH

PAP

YOU TELL RANMA SAOTOME...

THAT IF HE WANTS TO GET AKANE TENDO BACK...
OINK
HEY...

...HE MUST COME TO THE PLACE SHOWN ON THAT TICKET!
WAHAHAHAHA
OINK
B-BOING...
HEY, WAIT A MINUTE!

AKANE... HE THOUGHT THAT PIGGY WAS YOU!
HE'LL *PAY* FOR THAT!!
GRRRR

NIHAO, RANMA!
Shooting Gallery
50¢
YAY
HAHA
WHEE
HEY, SHAMPOO.
TINKLE
RANMA COME DATE WITH SHAMPOO!
SORRY, I GOTTA GO RESCUE AKANE.
IT'S NOT ME!
WHAT A MAROON, CALLIN' ME OUT TO A PLACE LIKE THIS...

SPECIAL INVITATION TO CHINESE ACROBAT CIRCUS SHOW?
AIYAAA!
ADMIT 1
CHINESE ACROBAT CIRCUS SHOW

SHAMPOO GET SENT SAME TICKET.
HUH?

PLEASE DO COME! THESE REAL CHINESE ACROBAT CIRCUS FROM CHINA!
CHINESE ACROBATS
WHEE
FAMILY FUN
YAY
WEIRD. I DON'T KNOW ANYBODY IN THE...
IT'S BEEN A LONG TIME, RANMA SAOTOME...
WHA--?
HEH HEH HEH HEH HEH

TONIGHT'S SHOW SHOULD BE VERY ENTERTAINING.
HEH HEH HEH HEH HEH
Y-YOU'RE--
AIYAAA! MOUSSE!
OINK
RANMA SAOTOME...
UNTIL I WIN BACK SHAMPOO FROM YOU...
I SHALL KEEP AKANE TENDO A HOSTAGE!
STOP SQUEEZING HER! YOU'RE MAKING HER CRY!
OINK
WHAP
DO TELL WHY YOU THINK THAT LOOKS LIKE AKANE TENDO.

EH?
POP
AAAH! WHEN DID THIS HAPPEN?!
OINK
HE HAVE BAD EYESIGHT. LIKE ALWAYS.
GONNNNNG
YAAAAAAAY!
TEEHEE HEE HEE HEE HEE
CLAP CLAP CLAP CLAP CLAP CLAP CLAP CLAP
CLAP CLAP CLAP CLAP
WE LUCKY TO GET FREE TICKET!
WOW, THAT'S AMAZING!

BAH.
LAUGH WHILE YOU CAN...
...UNTIL YOUR DEATH...
GLINT
RANMA SAOTOME!
CLAP CLAP CLAP CLAP CLAP CLAP
NOW WE NEEDING YOUR HELP!
CHNK CHNK
ONE MEMBER OF AUDIENCE, PLEASE COME STAGE!

FOR BRAVE VOLUNTEER, WE GIVE THIS PRIZE!
OINK
AH!!

RANMA, WOULD YOU KINDLY...
AKANE! WHAT'RE YOU DOING THERE?

BOOT
CUT IT OUT?!

OKAY, WE HAVE VOLUNTEER NOW!
VUUIP
HAH!
VRRRR
OOOH!
CLAP CLAP
CLAP
CLAP
CLAP CLAP
TOK
KLAK
KLAK

HUH ?
NOW, WHAT IS FATE OF POOR CAPTURED GIRL!?
RATTLE
DUM DE DUM DUM!

TAK TAK TAK
!
GLINT
YOW !!
TAK TAK TAK
OOOOOOO !
AIYAA.
WHAT THE... ?

IS ENTRANCE OF OUR BIG STAR!
KLANK
HUF HUF HUF

YAAAAY!!
WELCOME PLEASE MU MU-CHAN, THE DUCK!
TH-THIS AIN'T NO ORDINARY DUCK...
AND WHAT A DUCK!
HEH
UH-OH!
FWAP
FWAP

TAK TAK TAK DAK
YAAAY!
THAT CHICK'S JUST AS GOOD AS THE DUCK!
TUK
WHY... YOU... WEB-FOOTED...
Ptui!
FWAP
GEH!
KSSSS

KABOOM!
BOMBS...?!
POP POP POP POP POP POP
POP POP POP POP POP POP

KOFF
KOFF

HUH ?!

THEY'RE GONE! WHAT MAGIC!
OOOOOH!!
CLAP CLAP CLAP CLAP CLAP CLAP
CLAP CLAP CLAP CLAP CLAP CLAP

I THOUGHT SO! THAT DUCK WAS YOU!
CLAP CLAP CLAP CLAP CLAP CLAP CLAP CLAP CLAP CLAP CLAP CLAP CLAP

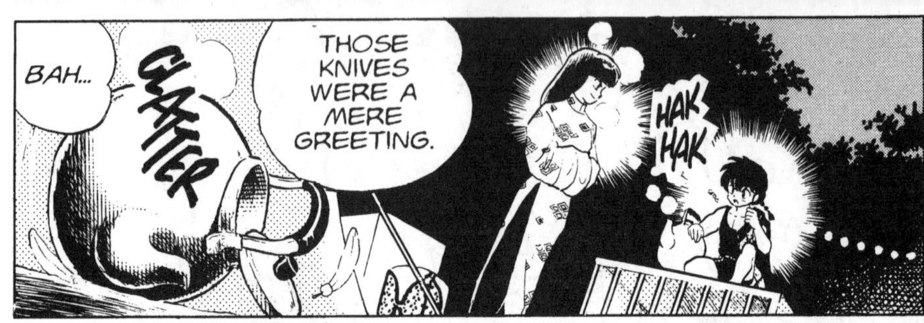
THOSE KNIVES WERE A MERE GREETING.
BAH...
CLATTER
HAK HAK

I'LL MAKE SURE I ENJOY IT!
SINCE YOU WENT TO THE TROUBLE GIVING ME THIS TICKET...
KOFF
ADMIT ONE

PREPARE YOURSELF, RANMA SAOTOME!
THE CIRCUS FROM HELL IS JUST BEGINNING!

PART 12
DUCK, RANMA, DUCK!

HWOOOOOOO
DO YOU KNOW...
GLUG
...WHAT THIS IS, RANMA?
WATER... ?

SEVERAL MONTHS AGO IN CHINA...
IT IS THE FRUIT OF MY LABORS!
IT IS NO ORDINARY WATER.
HERE SIR, IS LEGENDARY TRAINING GROUND OF CURSED SPRING, JUSENKYO.
SPSH
SPSH
I SHALL TRAIN ATOP THESE BAMBOO POLES FOR THE DEFEAT OF RANMA SAOTOME!
FWIP
AND SO I TOOK MY FIRST GLORIOUS STEP TO VICTORY!
AIYAAA! YOU FALL IN YAHZU-NIICHUAN!
BLOOSH
GLORIOUS, HUH?

SPRING OF DROWNED DUCK HAVE TRAGIC STORY OF DUCK WHAT DROWN THERE 1300 YEAR AGO...

BURBL

BRBL

NOW, WHOEVER FALL IN SAME SPRING...

CHOMP

BOP BOP
BITE ME, WILL YOU, RANMA !?
EEEEK!
OH, GET REAL !

EH ?
POP

SKRITCH SKRITCH SKRITCH

SO...
WHRRR...

YOU SAY THIS WATER IS THE FRUIT OF YOUR LABORS?
SPLASH
EYAAA!

HWOOOOOO
KLATTER

QUITE A JUMP.
THAT MEANS THIS WATER MUST BE...

BLOOP!
THAT'S RIGHT.
IT IS THE WATER...

...FROM THE SPRING OF THE DROWNED DUCK!
WHAT THE--?
POP
POP

MOUSSE!

KWAK

SHAMPOO...

SHAMPOO NO LET YOU HURT RANMA!

VIP

BONK

SHAMPOO HAVE NO INTENTION OF DATE WITH YOU!

HUH ?

GRRRR

BOING
FWAPPA
WHOA!
TAK
TAK TAK
COME 'N GET ME!
FWAP
HAHA
WHEE
VROOOOM
TAK
TAK
SHH SHH

FWAP
DOESN'T HE EVER RUN OUT ?!

SHAA

POP
POP
EEP!
POP
YAKI
GOLDFI

SPLAT
LOOK OUT!
PLISH PLOSH
GOLD FISH CATCH ¥50
LET'S TRY IT!
HEY! DUCK CATCHING!
OH DEAR DEAR ME...
QUAK QUAK QUAK
CHK CHK
HEY...
MOUSSE! WHY YOU--!
PINWHEEL

I'VE HAD *ENOUGH* OF YOUR STUPID GRUDGE!
VRRR
POIT
POIT
POIT
POIT

IF YOU WEREN'T SUCH A MORON...
BZZ BZZ
GWAK GWAK

...I WOULDN'T HAVE SHAMPOO PESTERIN' ME ALL THE--
BONK.

SHAMPOO WAS WORRIED ABOUT YOU...
SH-SHAMPOO...
SLOSH

NOW SHAMPOO MAD!
VROOM
YAAAAAH!!
BLOOSH
MYOW! MYOW! MYOW!
......

STRANGE.
WHERE DID EVERYONE GO?

WHAT ?!
HEH HEH HEH HEH
HEH HEH HEH HEH

WHAP WHAP WHAP WHAP
EEEEEK! A MONSTER !

AKANE TENDO...
EEEEEK!

FEH...
HM? OH, MOUSSE. IT'S YOU.
HUF HUF

OHHHHHH..

BOOOP

SHP

THIS TIME I HAVE YOU FOR SURE!

BIG CHINESE ACROBATIC MAGIC SHOW START VERY SOON!
WHIRRRRRR...
WHAT'S THIS? A GIRL THAT BECOMES A DUCK?
Amazing Duck Girl!
THE REAL THING!
HEY, SHE'S CUTE.
HUH?
VROOOOOM
AAAAARGH!
MOW! MOW!

YOWR!
SPLAT
FLUTTER FLUTTER
FUMP

END OF RANMA 1/2 VOLUME 8.